Molly
and the
Slow Teeth

D0962861

Molly and the Slow Teeth

by Pat Ross

pictures by Jerry Milord

SCHOLASTIC INC.
New York Toronto London Auckland Sydney

No part of this publication may be reproduced in whole or in part, or stored in a retrieval system, or transmitted in any form or by any means, electronic, mechanical, photocopying, recording, or otherwise, without written permission of the publisher. For information regarding permission, write to Lothrop, Lee & Shepard Books, a division of William Morrow & Company, 105 Madison Avenue, New York, N.Y. 10016.

ISBN 0-590-31950-7

Text copyright © 1980 by Pat Ross. Illustrations copyright © 1980 by Jerome E. Milord. All rights reserved. This edition is published by Scholastic Inc., 730 Broadway, New York, NY 10003, by arrangement with Lothrop, Lee & Shepard Books, a division of William Morrow & Company, Inc.

12 11 10 9 8 7 6 5 4 3 2   11   6 7 8 9/8 0 1/9

Printed in the U.S.A.   11

For Erica, with love

ONE

Molly Davis had not lost one tooth yet. And she was already in second grade.

She checked her teeth for loose ones every day.

She tried to wiggle the big top teeth.

Not a budge!

She tried to push the little bottom teeth.

Stuck tight!

"You've just got slow teeth," her
mother said. "They'll come out when
they're ready."

"Be glad you have a fast brain," joked her father.

Jokes did not help. Nothing helped.

9

Everybody else in her class had spaces where teeth used to be.

Everybody else had their name on the Tooth Chart in the front of the room.

Only Molly's name was missing.

Marvin Wilson had the fastest teeth in the class. His name was on the Tooth Chart eight times. He already had five grown-up teeth.

He counted them every day. "One, two . . ." Marvin would begin to count.

He pointed and counted out loud. Molly covered her ears before he got to "five."

Susan Steinberg was Molly's best friend. Susan had a special tooth pillow with a tiny pocket on top that said "MY TOOTH."

One day, Susan held it up for Molly to see.

"That makes *four*!" said Molly when she saw another tooth.

"We can share the pillow," offered Susan.

It was hard for Molly to share a pillow that had somebody else's tooth inside.

Susan got to put her name on the Tooth Chart first thing the next day at school.

TOOTH CHART

My Name	Date	How I Lost It
MARVIN	OcTober 10	SLEEPING
Phil	OCTOBER 13	Eating DINNER
ERICA	NOVEMBER 8	Jumping in GYM
SUSAN	NOVEMBER 12	I PULLED IT!

Molly didn't feel like being best friends with Susan that day.

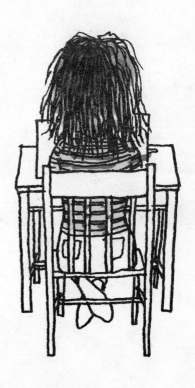

The next morning, Molly colored her front tooth black with a marker. She did not smile at breakfast.

At school, Molly found Susan right away. "Look, no tooth!" she said. She pointed to her black tooth.

Susan made a face. "Disgusting!" said Susan.

Molly had to brush ten times to get off all the black.

TWO

That night, Molly had a plan to fool the Tooth Fairy.

She put a stone under her pillow. It was small and white, and shaped just like a tooth.

"I hope the Tooth Fairy checks tonight," Molly called to her mother.

"Don't worry," her mother said. "The Tooth Fairy works very late, so sweet dreams."

The next morning, Molly found a shiny dime under her pillow. There was also a note.

At breakfast, Molly told her mother,
"I hope I'm not too old for the Tooth
Fairy when it's time."

"You won't be," said her mother. "Trust me."

"I know more about the Tooth Fairy than you think," said Molly. "Maybe I know too much."

"I won't tell," said her mother. "It can be our Tooth Fairy secret."

At school, Molly tried to keep her mind off her teeth. But even the lunch milk made her think of strong teeth.

Molly played with her front teeth during math class. After class, Marvin told Molly about a way to pull teeth. You only needed a string and a doorknob. She had lots of both at home.

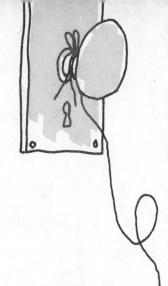

Before dinner, Molly picked a big top tooth.

She tied one end of the string to her tooth. She tied the other end to a doorknob.

Marvin said all you had to do was slam the door hard. *Zip*—the tooth would pop out. But Marvin did not say if it hurt.

Just then, Molly's father walked by. "Looks like somebody tied you up," he said.

"No jokes today," said Molly.

"Hurting your mouth is no joke," her father said.

"That's just what I was thinking," said Molly.

Together they untied the tooth and the doorknob.

At bedtime, her top tooth felt very sore. She asked her mother to test it.

"I can't tell," said her mother. "Maybe it's sore from so much testing."

"I'll never lose a tooth!" cried Molly. "I'll be a grown-up with baby teeth! I'm never checking my dumb, tight, slow teeth again—ever!"

Molly cried hard into her pillow until she finally fell asleep.

TYRANNOSAURUS REX

THREE

Molly did not check her teeth for almost a week.

That was the week they learned all about dinosaurs. Molly loved science class that week.

Then one day, Marvin asked about dinosaur teeth. That made Molly think about her own teeth.

She pushed the bottom teeth with her tongue.

Still stuck like glue!

Then she tried the top teeth.

One wiggled!

No doubt about it! Molly had a loose tooth. She could hardly believe it.

Molly's tooth got looser and looser. It wiggled and it wobbled. Then it bent all the way back. Molly could even twist it around. But still that tooth *would not* come out.

Day after day, all her friends helped test the tooth. Day after day, Molly and her friends waited.

One day at lunch, everybody was acting silly. Susan said, "Have some dinosaur, my dear!"

Marvin said, "Don't talk with your mouth full. It attracts dinosaurs!"

Everybody laughed.

Then Molly pretended to be a hungry dinosaur. She roared and she snorted. Then she took a big bite of her apple. Everybody really laughed at that!

Molly stopped acting silly. "Who put rocks in my apple?" she asked.

Everybody stopped roaring and snorting.

Molly reached into her mouth and pulled out something small and white.

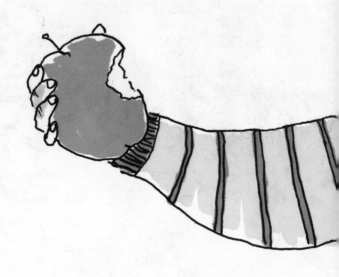

"Your tooth!" cried Susan.

"*Some* rock," said Marvin.

Molly stuck her tongue through the space where the tooth used to be. It felt soft and empty and wonderful.

"Well," said Molly to her tooth, "you sure took your time."

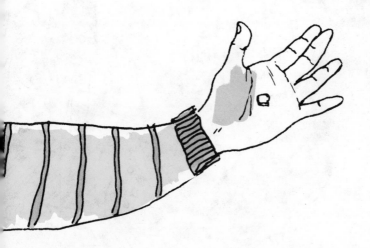

The next morning, the tooth was still under her pillow. Next to it were a quarter and a note.

Molly dressed fast. She didn't want to be late for school.

Tooth Chart time came first. And Molly knew that a place on the Tooth Chart was waiting just for her.

SUSAN   NOVEMBER 12

MOLLY   NOVEMBER 28

About the Author

Pat Ross, a children's book editor in New York City, is the author of several books for young people, including *Meet M and M* and *What Ever Happened to the Baxter Place?* The inspiration for this book, she tells us, came from her daughter Erica, "whose first loose tooth became the most important thing in her life."

About the Artist

Jerry Milord, a former advertising artist, made his children's book debut with *Maggie and the Goodbye Gift* in collaboration with his wife, Sue. Now living in Texas, he continues to charm readers of all ages with his unique style.